Belle
of the
Ball

Created by Keith Chapman

First published in Great Britain by HarperCollins Children's Books in 2006

1 3 5 7 9 10 8 6 4 2 ISBN: 0-00-721363-8

Based on the television series *Fifi and the Flowertots*
and the original script 'Belle of the Ball' by Diane Redmond.
© Chapman Entertainment Limited 2006

Printed and bound in China

Belle of the Ball

HarperCollins *Children's Books*

It was a bright
summer's day in
Flowertot Garden.
Fifi was visiting Poppy's
Market Stall, where she
met Violet and
Aunt Tulip.

"Hello Aunt Tulip," Fifi waved.
"What are you doing at the market?"

"Sweet Potatoes Child!
I'm getting ready for tonight's
Midsummer Flowertot Ball," she replied.

"Buttercups and Daisies! I forgot!"
Fifi said, as the others laughed.

"What are you going to wear?"
Violet asked.

"Oh I don't know," Fifi laughed,
"I'm far too busy to worry
about dressing up. It's
what you feel like, not
what you look like
that is important."

"Don't you care what you look like at all, Fifi?" asked Violet. Before Fifi could answer, she was interrupted by the sound of a scooter.

It was Pip.

"Ahem," he started, looking as if he had something very important to say. "Primrose wants some silk, satin, sequins and lace for her Flowertot ball gown,".

Poppy gathered up all the things Primrose needed from her stall. "I think Primrose wants to win the best dressed medal," she chuckled.

"I'd better get going," smiled Fifi.

"Can I come with you, Fifi? I need your help," whispered Pip.

"I want to look good for the ball,"
began Pip, "but I don't know what to wear."
Fifi looked thoughtful for a moment. "What
about wearing a cloak and you can go as Pip
Prince Charming," she suggested.
"I like that!" beamed Pip, "I'll go and see
what I can find!"
With that, he hurried off.

Back in her garden, Fifi found Bumble
holding up a stripy tie and a bow tie.

"Bouncing Buttercups, Fifi!"

he buzzed excitedly. "I don't know what to
wear tonight!"

"Not you too, Bumble," Fifi sighed.
"But which tie should I wear?"
Bumble asked.

"They're both nice. I
know, go and ask
Primrose. She always
knows what's good
to wear."

"Good idea!" said
Bumble and buzzed
off happily.

Over in the apple house, Stingo was showing his Flowertot ball invitation to Slugsy. "There'll be strawberries, ice-cream, pies and homemade cakes – not to mention lollipops!"

"I'm ssso excited about the ball!" said Slugsy.
"But **you** can't go to a ball like **that!**"
Stingo said, shaking his head.
Slugsy looked very disappointed. "How elssse can
I go, SSStingo?" he asked.
"Oh slug of very little brain! You have to dress up!"
said Stingo. He looked hard at Slugsy. "And we're
going to need a lot of material to cover you!"

Back in her garden, Fifi was hard
at work when Pip came running
towards her, clutching some bright
blue feathers.
"Oh Fifi, look what I've got!" he yelled excitedly.
"Blue jay feathers! Pip, they're beautiful." Fifi said.
"I'll go and buy some ribbon from the market
and we'll make you a spendid cloak."
But Fifi wasn't the only one
going to market.
Just as she arrived,
Stingo buzzed
towards the stall.

Buzzzzzzzzzzzzzzzz!

"I'm looking for some material Poppy. In fact – I'm looking for a lot of material," he said. "It's a surprise for Slugsy," he whispered to Fifi.

"I hope it's a nice surprise, Stingo," Fifi said sternly.

"On my wasp's honour, it's a very nice surprise!" said Stingo as he buzzed off.

Soon, Slugsy was draped in the bright, red material.

"Do I look pretty, SSStingo?" Slugsy posed for his friend.

"No!" said Stingo, "but at least it covers you."

"Will you dance with me?" Slugsy asked, dipping in a huge curtsey. "We've got to practissse or we won't be able to dance at the ball."

"I'm not dancing with a slug!" cried Stingo. Slugsy gave Stingo his sweetest look. "Oh, alright then," Stingo agreed.

"Laaah, laaah, laaah," sang Slugsy, as he dragged Stingo around the terrace in a bumpy waltz.

"Oh, Rotten Raspberries!" grumbled Stingo.

It was almost time for the ball and Pip and Fifi were making his outfit. In no time at all, Pip had a handsome blue jay feather cloak, tied to his shoulders by a beautiful purple ribbon.

"Thank you Fifi, see you at the Flowertot ball!" Pip said.

"Bye bye, handsome Pip Prince Charming," waved Fifi.

Pip had barely left the garden when Bumble buzzed in, flourishing a flashy bow tie. "I've decided to wear this one, Fifi!" he said.

"And you should see Primrose's dress, it's gorrrrrr-geous."

"Fussing over clothes is very silly," Fifi said to herself as Bumble buzzed off. "but if everyone else is making an effort to look their best..."

Fifi looked down at her dungarees. "What should I wear?"

She plopped down on the ground and looked around her garden until her eyes landed on the lovely flowers all around her.

"Buttercups and Daisies!" she laughed. "I've had a fantastic Flowertot idea!"

Later that evening, Fifi arrived at the Flowertot Midsummer Ball. Everyone turned and stared, at her beautiful ball gown made entirely from flower petals!

"Will you dance with me, Princess Fifi?" asked Pip with a deep bow.

"With pleasure, Pip Prince Charming!" giggled Fifi.

All the Flowertots began to dance around Fifi and Pip, except for Stingo and Slugsy. They were far too busy feasting on the cakes, jellies, sandwiches and lollipops!

It didn't take long before Stingo and
Slugsy began to feel a little sick.

"My tummy hurts!" groaned Slugsy as they
tried to sneak off while everyone was dancing.

"And where are you two going?" asked Fifi.

"Home, we feel sick," moaned Stingo. They both
looked terrible!

"Fiddly Flowerpetals!
If you hadn't been so
greedy you could have
stayed and danced all
night," Fifi said, watching
them stagger off.

"We'll remember
that next time,"
Stingo muttered.

"You all look so beautiful." Aunt Tulip had started her speech. It was time to announce the winner of the best dressed Flowertot medal!

"But somebody's got to win, so the best dressed medal goes to Pip for his fabulous blue cloak!" Aunt Tulip smiled and handed the medal to Pip as everyone clapped and cheered.

"Thank you!" Pip said,
"but if it weren't for Fifi, I
wouldn't have had anything to wear
to the ball so I'm going to give my medal to Fifi
Forget-Me-Not!"

Pip carefully placed the medal around Fifi's neck. "Because not only is she kind, she's also the Flowertot Belle of the Ball!"

"Thank you!" she blushed as everyone clapped and cheered for Fifi Forget-Me-Not, Flowertot Belle of the Ball.

Make Your Own Flowertot Ball Invitations

Next time you're having a party, why not make some lovely Flowertot invitations like these!

To make 10 invitations you will need:

* Yellow cardboard
* Green cardboard
* Lots of different coloured tissue paper
* A coloured pen to write with
* Glue
* Safety scissors
* Some ribbon
* A grown-up to help!

1. Carefully cut out a circle of yellow cardboard and write on the date, time and place of your party. Ask a grown-up to help so it's neat and pretty.

2. Cut a small hole in the top of the yellow card.

3. Tear the tissue paper up into lots of petal shapes then glue them all around the outside of the yellow card to make a lovely flower.

4. Cut a stalk and a leaf out of the green card and stick them to the back of the yellow card.

5. Thread some pretty ribbon through the hole you made in the middle of the card and tie it in a loop. Now your friend can hang up the pretty invitation!